WINTER SOLSTICE WISHES

A ROGUES INC. SHORT STORY

GAYLE PARNESS

FOREWORD

Dear Readers & Rogues,

This short story is about two of the characters from the Rogues Shifter Series: Sasha, who's been with the series since **Rebirth**, and Elle, who we met in **Cut Off**. Because the heat level is much higher than in my original YA series, I consider this story to be an adult read. Sasha and Elle are way past young adulthood. In case you're keeping track of the timeline, this is book 7.5 in the Rogues Shifter Series, but it can be read on its own.

Winter Solstice Wishes first appeared in the 2014 holiday anthology, Candy Cane Kisses and Magical Embraces. This anthology is no longer available for purchase.

Elle, a fae female, has refused to return to the Faerie Court because of the treatment she endured under the former queen, Fionna. She's been a guest in Sasha's home for the last few months, and is finally beginning to feel comfortable in this new world—finding herself drawn to the gentle warrior, but not feeling worthy to stand at his side. When she sees how Sasha has decorated his home for Christmas, Elle invites him to celebrate the winter solstice with her.

Sasha, a vampire with a violent past, is completely smitten by this sweetly elegant female, but he has many demons of his own to dispel. When Elle invites him to a magical celebration, he jumps at the chance to spend time with her. But can they heal each other on the Winter Solstice, the longest night of the year?

PROLOGUE

Faerie after the fall of Queen Fionna

Elle

W hen I heard the squeak of the bedroom door opening, I jumped to my feet and wiped the tears from my eyes. I must not seem weak. My dagger was already in hand, hidden in the folds of my skirt. This time I was certain I could muster the courage to die with honor. But it was a male I did not know who entered, one whose voice I did not recognize.

"Do not be afraid, child," he said in rich tones. "No one will hurt you now that I have returned. Garrett and his family have requested you leave Faerie and accompany them to the Mortal Plain so that you may find peace away from court. I have agreed, although I am saddened that you may decide never to return."

He was standing in the shadows, so I could not see his face, yet my skin prickled with the effect of his power. "Step into the light," I demanded, my blade shaking along with my hand.

The moment he did, I collapsed to the floor, the shock of seeing this male forcing the breath from my lungs. Finvarra, the former King of Faerie stood in my dank and barren room. He and Queen Aine had abandoned the people of Faerie centuries ago. His disappearance was the reason his daughter, Fionna, had taken the crown. My suffering under her rule had been as much this royal's responsibility as Fionna's, yet because of his unparalleled magic, I could not carry through with my plan to attack whomever next entered my room. I'd hoped to die in the attempt, which would have suited me well.

Now it appeared I would be forced to live outside of Faerie until I healed. I cast my eyes downward in deference and embarrassment. There would be no healing for me.

"Stand, child." I did. "What is your name?" he asked.

"Elle, sire."

"Follow me, Elle." The king spoke with great gentleness, the tone a balm spreading warmth throughout my body. "I will find you a suitable room where you may wash and eat. Then perhaps you will name the males or females who hurt you? I will see to them personally and they will not go unpunished."

"Thank you, sire."

"You will be leaving with Garrett and Jacqueline in a few hours, but only if you agree to go. No one will force you."

No one will force you. Could this be true? For so many months I'd wished to die. But I'd watched a vampire fight with all his strength to live, battling blood loss and the effects of torture, keeping alive to finally be rescued by his mate, his son and his friends. A shiver raised the hairs on my arms and legs as I remembered how I also had fought against my torturers at first. My hope had died quickly. I'd been weak.

I followed my king to the nicer room and sat down to eat when he asked me to, although I could taste nothing. Whether I was in the Mortal Plain or Faerie did not matter. No one could rescue me from my memories.

1

SASHA

The week before Christmas in Crescent City, California

Sasha

Elle walked down the stairs, her blue gown brushing each step as she passed, her natural grace a gift to my senses. When she reached the bottom step, she frowned. "Sasha, why have you brought a tree into your home?"

Rick and I were enjoying a beer, having just lowered the enormous fir tree into the stand and adjusting it to Rick's specifications. Holidays didn't mean much to me, but because Rick enjoyed Christmas, I humored him. Like any part-time yuletide participant, I made myself scarce when it was time to hang the lights, but even I had to admit decorating the tree on Christmas Eve, inviting our friends to join in, and making the occasion into a party was worth all the effort.

In a few quick strides Elle had reached the tree. She crouched and leaned forward, placing her hand on the trunk where it met the tree stand. "You have chopped it down?"

Neither Rick or I could have predicted the look of horror she aimed at me. "It's a tradition," I said, the words tumbling out in my defense. "The tree doesn't go to waste. Sinlae uses it for compost after the holidays." Sinlae was a demi-fey who along with her mates, took care of our gardens. I thought maybe the idea that we were helping the environment would unruffle some of Elle's lovely feathers, but in preparation for worst, I swallowed the last of my beer. Elle had a temper.

"Hmph. To some residents of Faerie it would be seen as a killing offense." Head bent, she mumbled a few words in her musical language, rising when she'd finished. She peeked out the bay window and asked, "But where do you hold your winter solstice ceremony? It is tonight. We must make preparations."

Rick stood, gesturing in a gentlemanly way that she should join us. "Would you like a glass of wine, Lady Elle?" The smile she directed *his* way was bright and friendly. Guess I shouldn't tell her Rick was the one who'd wielded the ax. He owed me one, but then I owed him my life a dozen times over.

"Thank you, Heinrich. I appreciate your thoughtfulness, but I have no need of refreshment at the moment." She glided to the chair beside mine, sitting as elegantly as she did all things in life. I could watch her move and listen to her speak for hours and never feel the need to do anything else.

Rick chuckled, breaking my sublime meditation by loudly gathering our beer bottles and tossing them in the recycle bin. As usual, he'd caught me staring at her like a love-struck teen. I glared at him in warning, hoping to discourage any jibes. Rick's taunts were getting old.

"*You need to ask her out, Sash. Your simpering stares are giving me shingles.*" Because we were vampires in the same nest, we could communicate mind-to-mind, a handy gift in all circumstances, but particularly when you were being ridiculed by your BFF.

My glare dissolved, a resigned huff taking its place. "*I'm not in her class.*" Fae ladies did not date vampires who over the centuries had murdered hundreds of humans and other supernaturals. Granted, I hadn't been given any choice, but that didn't pardon even one death.

"*If I hear that excuse one more time, I'm going to decorate the tree with your toes.*"

"*Real festive.*"

Elle, who was used to our mental ping ponging, was still waiting patiently for an answer to her question. I sat up straighter, explaining, "Vampires don't celebrate the solstice. That's a fae thing."

She wrinkled her forehead, the lines adding shading to the smooth plains of her skin. My fingers twitched, eager to hold a sketchpad and a stick of charcoal, although any attempt at capturing her radiant glow would fail. "But were you not once human? Human groups enjoy solstice festivals, do they not?" She turned to Rick for confirmation, ignoring me.

Back on the couch, Rick put his feet up on the coffee table. Elle arched an eyebrow and his feet hit the floor. She never scolded Rick, mostly because he didn't behave like a *dungeon dweller*, the phrase she'd recently begun using for me. We both wanted to please her, but I'd often do things I knew would rile her up. My world was complete whenever

Elle scolded me, frowned at me, laughed with me, smiled at me—noticed me.

"My family always celebrated Weihnachten, or Christmas as humans call it here," Rick explained. Having been made vampire only fifty years ago, Rick's German accent still flavored his English and a lot of his American girlfriends-slash-blood donors found it *adorable*. Rick was six foot eight inches and three hundred pounds—not exactly adorable in my estimation. But then who was I to judge?

I scanned Elle's lovely lines, her delicate features strengthened by courage and determination, her pale skin glowing with warm shades in the firelight. I wanted so badly to paint her portrait, but she'd refused, saying she wouldn't have time to tend to her duties if she spent hours posing for a picture she'd be embarrassed for anyone to see.

Despite her difficult past, I wouldn't have painted her as a vulnerable maiden, a victim or a servant, even if most of the world saw her that way. To my eyes Elle was a warrior, a female who'd survived the worst and battled her way back.

I cleared my throat, wanting Elle's attention back on me. "My family didn't have time for special holidays because we were too busy trying to stay alive. Winters in Russia were the worst." I'd been forced into the tsar's army, trudging through snow up to my thighs so that we could breach the next hill and destroy another village. I still had nightmares about that time, although they were less frequent since our beautiful house guest from Faerie arrived. Now my dreams were all about her.

Elle ignored me. Again. "And what was Christmas like for you, Heinrich?"

"I remember—"

"Why do you always call us by our full names?" I asked a little too loudly.

Elle's chin jutted in irritation. "It is a sign of respect, as is not interrupting your friend when he is speaking."

I did my best to look sheepish—not my forte. "Is Elle short for something?"

"Elle is not my full name. It is the name I was given by Queen Fionna when I served her at court." She looked past me to the window, her eyes glazing over. The pain of her time at court was still evident. "It is not a proper name for a lady of Faerie."

"You've lived in our house for six months and you've never told me your full name? Why?"

Her violet gaze pinned me to my chair. "Because you have not earned the right to address me in that way."

Her attempts to put me in my place were a game I enjoyed on so many levels, but there was something hurtful about this last comment. "I like the name Elle. It's sweet, like you."

I'd caught her off guard, but the frown returned with a blink of her large eyes. "Which only proves you are feeble-minded. I am not sweet."

I ignored Rick's laughter and leaned closer to Elle, almost within touching distance. I lowered my voice, adding a hint of huskiness. "I can't argue the point, since you haven't allowed me to taste you." I made sure my grin showed off the tips of my fangs.

Elle pretended to be offended, tossing her head in a sexy way that made her dark waves dance around her shoulders. I'd spent many a sleepless day fantasizing about fisting my hands in that lovely hair as I bit into her neck, taking in the most delicious of all nectars. Fae blood held powerful magic, but my craving was more specific. I'd happily turn my back on a houseful of fae, instead crawling on my hands and knees to beg this female, the one who'd been diving me mad for six months, to offer me one delicious drop. Or better yet, some romantic time alone with her.

Elle and I were still only inches apart and she was fighting back a smile with everything she had, the proof in the tiny creases around her large eyes. I'd grown to love those smile-induced lines. My only wish was to see them more often.

"Did you happen to notice the plant I hung over the doorway?" I asked, moving on to another subject that might make her smile.

Heinrich chuckled, holding up his hands and shaking his head. "That was his idea."

She looked where I was pointing. "Yellow mischief? Is there some significance?"

"We call it mistletoe and hang it above somewhere a beautiful woman might stand. If we catch her there we're allowed to kiss her."

Her giggle brought on happy creases. "You are a cad, Sasha Vodinski, to trap a female in such a way."

I leaned back, the music of her laughter still singing in my ears. Elle had been through hell and back at the fae court, used and tortured by Queen Fionna's sycophants. Although she rarely spoke about her experiences, she'd chosen not to return to Faerie even though King Finvarra, a gentler ruler, had reclaimed his crown and Fionna had disappeared. However, Elle was a subject of Faerie, staying with us by the king's grace. If he told her to return, she'd have no choice but to obey him.

With nowhere else to place her, Garrett, the head of our nest, had suggested she move in with Rick and me, telling us about her life at court and making sure we understood how fragile she was. The first month was tough: hearing her cry but not able to do anything to help her, sending up food that was rarely eaten. But then one evening she'd walked downstairs, rolled up her sleeves and begun to wash the wine glasses we'd left in the sink.

Like most households, we had an appliance that took care of that job, but Rick and I were way too startled to speak, staying where we were so we didn't scare her back into hiding. When she'd finished, she sat in the wingback chair across from us, her lyrical words enchanting me. It was the first time I'd ever heard her speak, the first time I'd been close to her, the first time I'd known she was mine.

"I APOLOGIZE FOR MY BEHAVIOR. *I have been an unworthy house guest who has not shown proper gratitude for your kindness and your patience. Sinlae has scolded me on several occasions and I am determined that I will not continue to shame my people by behaving like a child. From now until the time I am sent away, I will assist Sinlae in the gardens and I will also help you tend to your lovely home in the hopes that my service will make up for my early misdeeds."*

DESPITE OUR INSISTING that her status as our guest did not include the duties of a servant, she'd stubbornly done as she'd promised, keeping our world clean and organized, weaving her faerie spell into my heart with every graceful movement, small smile and musical laugh. She'd bewitched me without a hint of magic and I'd welcomed each moment I spent wrapped in her spell.

What made me happiest was how staying with us was helping her heal. A small crack had worked its way up the wall she'd erected to protect herself after the horrors of her life at the Faerie Court. I figured if I just kept chipping away, gently, steadily, she'd let it crumble. And then, who knew? I couldn't wait to find out.

Rick laughed again, bringing me back to the present. "As I was saying before Sash interrupted, I remember holiday celebrations in Munich. We would eat sausages and roast goose, exchange presents, and drink winterbrau. As a child, during Advent our parents would fill stockings with small gifts and candy. Christmas was an opportunity to spend time with family members you hadn't seen for many months."

"Sounds cool." I shrugged and turned away, suddenly jealous that I didn't have any happy holiday memories. My family had died of influenza while I'd been with the army killing innocents in some border village, all because the tsar and his generals wanted the territory. I found out later that local soldiers had burned my parents' and sisters' bodies along with our family cottage.

I still missed the sound of Mama working in the kitchen, her hands and clothing scented with the comforting smells of cooking food. My younger sisters would tease me often, giggling over a scheme they'd planned or joking about some girl I had a crush on. I missed them, too.

When I looked up again, Elle's gaze pierced mine, as if she could see into my troubled soul. "We will make memories tonight. You will come with me into the forest to celebrate the winter solstice." She smiled at Rick. "You may also accompany us, Heinrich."

He winked at me and stood. "Sorry. Hot date. But thanks." He'd be going to one of the donor clubs in Gasquet to feed. He treated his females like queens, buying them gifts and protecting them from other, more violent vampires. In return, they fussed over him like a harem over their maharaja and called him *adorable*. Rick often boasted that he wasn't a one-woman male, and his stable seemed to accept that fact. I suspected he just hadn't met the right female.

Now me, on the other hand, I was pretty sure the female I was meant to spend my very long life with was currently living in my house and sleeping in the bedroom next to mine. But she rarely met my gaze, except in irritation, and never came close enough to touch my skin, except by accident. Maybe accompanying her to the winter solstice celebration would widen that crack in her wall, or better yet, crumble it.

I jumped up. "I'm in!" Her eyebrow arched in dismay. "Forgive me." I swept my arm out and bowed like a courtier. "Lady Elle, I am honored by your invitation." When I rose and met her gaze she was smiling and shaking her head.

"You tease, but I will teach you manners yet, Master Vodinski."

Her eyes glittered with humor but she'd managed to pull off a snooty tone pretty well. She was playing with me for the first time. I lowered my voice and leaned closer. "I give you permission to teach me whatever you desire."

2

ELLE

The path I'd created wound between oak and fir, alder and pine, meadow and brush. By design, it was only wide enough for us to walk shoulder to shoulder, leaving little impact on the surrounding habitat. Alone together for the first time, Sasha's closeness was almost overwhelming, the delicious scent of him so strong it weakened my knees and speeded my heart beat.

How would I survive this night without throwing myself into his arms?

Tall like a fae lord, Sasha's long, well formed legs flowed upward, joining his body in a pleasing way, his stomach firm, his chest and arms radiating strength. I had seen him without a shirt when he trained with his weapons and also in his bathing attire when he enjoyed the oddly scented pool. When he participated in those activities I would sometimes hide so he would not see me admiring his male perfection. It would have shamed me to be seen, my skin flushed and hungry for his touch.

I wrapped my shawl more tightly around my shoulders, hiding my wanton smile by looking down at the ground. A rabbit scurried across our path, hurrying home before the snow began to fall. The evening sky had lost its stars to the dark clouds, the creatures of the forest instinctively understanding the possible danger.

"You cold?" he asked. "You can use my jacket."

His kind words drew my gaze to his face and I was once more stunned by his beautiful smile. Sasha was as handsome as any male I had seen, his smile easy and genuine, his lips designed for mine alone, if only that were possible. His startling light blue eyes spoke to my heart, and not simply because of their beauty. There was pain reflected there, born in a darkness I understood. Sasha did his best to block out his distressing memories, throwing himself into his work with the Rogues team and his security business, hiding his sorrow by staying busy. He used humor as a shield, work as a sword, fighting against the pain of his past with every blow.

My face was warming under his scrutiny. "I'm comfortable. Thank you, Sasha."

"I've been in these woods a hundred times, but I don't know this trail." He stopped, turning slowly in an attempt to get his bearings.

"I created it tonight. It will take us directly to the festival grounds."

"Cool trick." He pulled up the collar of his brown jacket to block the wind, which had picked up in strength during the last few minutes. "Too bad you can't change the weather."

Because I'd lined the path with dry moss, we made very little noise as we trod toward the celebration. We kept our conversations to a whisper, preferring not to frighten the smaller creatures through whose home we journeyed. Sasha had his hands in his pockets. He was shivering.

"I am surprised the cold bothers you." I had not thought to inquire about a vampire's ability to adjust to inclement weather. A fae can stand naked in a blizzard and not be affected.

"This kind of cold, with snow in the air, brings back bad memories. Can we take the ley lines?" he asked.

"I am not..." I shuffled my feet, hesitating. Admitting to weakness in front of this capable male was more difficult than I imagined. "I continue to heal, but there was much damage." And I had developed a fear of traveling the lines, a cowardly condition I could not admit to out loud. If I stepped into their energy my presence would be noticed and I might be called back to court. I tightened my shawl as I trembled, my mind taking me once more to those rooms, to those brutal males.

Sasha took my hand, immediately releasing it when he heard me gasp. He must have thought he'd frightened me. "I'm sorry. I shouldn't have touched you. You were shaking," he explained.

My blood warmed in my veins once more. His simple compassionate gesture had brought me back to the present, back to him. No one had cared about my well being since childhood. I extended my hand. "Please don't be distressed. I was only surprised at the sudden contact." He hesitated, unsure. To put him at ease, I smiled. "If we are holding hands I may be able to warm both of us."

"Another magical gift?" He smiled in return, wrapping my hand in his, raising it and kissing it gently. "It is my plea-sure to hold your hand, Lady Elle."

My heart thrummed at his words, matching the beat of the smaller woodland creatures I'd glimpsed along the way. I had once thought he mocked me, calling me lady, but I knew now he used the term with respect, perhaps even affection.

We had stopped for a moment near a group of fir trees, snow coating their needles and sparkling under the moonlight. "This is the first time we've been alone together." He spoke softly, taking small steps with words and deeds to gain my trust as one would a young child. He was always so careful with me, except for the times he teased. I liked those times best.

"Is it the first time? I had not realized." That was a lie. I had thought about little else since he said he would come with me to the festival.

He squeezed my hand playfully, perhaps sensing my untruth. I glanced away, embarrassed, but he tilted my chin so I'd have to gaze into his face. "I'll never hurt you, Elle."

I blinked back a tear. "You have given me no reason to fear you. I trust both you and Heinrich." But he did not understand how fragile my heart was when I was near him. A cruel action or unkind word from Sasha would hurt me more than anything that had gone before. I should never have allowed my heart to hope again.

He seemed satisfied by my answer, and happily, did not release my hand. Brushing a few snowflakes from his chest and shaking out his shoulder-length blond hair, he asked, "Does it snow in Faerie?"

"Only if someone wishes it to snow, which is rare."

"So you've never ice skated or ridden a sled or made a snow man or snow angels?"

"What is a snow angel?"

He looked at the ground. "We'd need more snow than this. Maybe I can show you later?"

"I would like that very much."

Snow dampened my uncovered head. I tried unsuccessfully to shake it off. He laughed, using the hand that wasn't joined to mine to brush my shoulders and comb through my hair. When his cool fingers stroked against my neck I shivered, but there was nothing icy about the gaze that met mine when I looked up.

He wanted to touch me again, but instead of moving closer his shoulders slumped. He scanned the path ahead of us. "Maybe we should hurry. Neither of us wants to spend the solstice as an ice sculpture."

Clutching his hand a little tighter, I searched the broad plains his face for answers. Snowflakes were landing on his cheeks, leaving trails and wet smudges as they melted against his warmer skin. His golden hair sparkled like the lightly coated trees surrounding us, a winter sight as lovely as any I had seen. In truth, I wanted nothing about this night to be hurried or rushed, but he had waited so patiently. "Yes. The festival will begin very soon."

We set out again, walking hand in hand, and I thought back to when I'd first come to meet my warrior. I'd been nervous, living in the same house with two unattached males, but there was never an instant when I felt unsafe. Although they knew what I was and what I had done, not once had Sasha or Heinrich treated me like a whore, trying to touch me or seduce me as if it was their right. Occasionally Sasha would tease me with flirty comments, but that was his way to get me to smile. And as I lay in my bed each night, I often wished he truly meant the sweet, sexy words he sometimes uttered in jest.

Sasha was a natural warrior, a male of strength, intelligence and honor. But I was not fit to be the lady of a warrior, nor any honorable male. Sinlae disagreed, but she was a demi-fey, a female pixie with three males who loved her dearly and kept her very happy. She was a queen in her own right and her world was not mine.

If I returned to Faerie, I would be shunned. Perhaps not by the more gentle-hearted of the Sidhe, but certainly by the families of the fae lords who'd used me. And there were many. So many. They would blame me for their father's or brother's or husband's actions, as if I'd seduced them into bed or begged these males to hurt me. They would never believe the truth and I would have to remain silent to survive.

How long before I slid into despair?

Gentle fingers brushed my shoulder, bringing me back to this night with this male. He'd noticed my distress and sought to offer comfort. In all my years, Sasha's was the only touch I'd ever wanted, his the only mouth I yearned to kiss, the only body I wished to see naked above my own.

My face heated like a young fae maiden's so I focused on the path ahead, hoping he had not noticed. His legs were longer, but he matched his pace to mine.

Minutes later, we arrived at the festival clearing, a space free of snow and wind, dotted with flowering berry bushes and gardens of winter roses and mums. In the center, a large bonfire glowed and sputtered, the smell of burning birch and elder branches bringing back happy childhood memories.

"Holy..."

I stopped his next words with my hand on his mouth. "Respect is key in this place, lowly vampire," I teased. "The forest allows us to stay and celebrate as long as we honor it with our words and our deeds."

Expecting his usual teasing retort, I was shocked when Sasha trapped my hand against his lips, taking in my scent with a long breath, his eyes beginning to sparkle with a silver light. With the lips I had dreamed about, he kissed my palm, running the tip of his tongue along the scars on my wrist. They were the ugly evidence of my years bound with iron, adding to my shame.

But Sasha was not disgusted. "So sweet," he said. "I knew you would be."

And the chains fell away.

I held her hand and waited, smiling, hoping she wouldn't run, praying she'd take it as innocent fun, even though the taste of her skin had spiked my desire.

She took a step back and I instantly released her hand. I'd never let her see me as a male who'd force his attentions on her like the males she'd had to submit to at court. I wanted to find those disgusting creatures and kill them slowly, but I was not allowed to visit Faerie and I doubted they would ever show their ugly faces here in Crescent City.

"Sasha..." she pouted, blinking several times. "Try to behave."

Scold me again, gentle lady, and I will be yours for all time.

"It's the solstice, right? I've heard about what goes on at these Faerie parties." Jackie and Garrett had attended a few *summer* solstice celebrations and had regaled us with stories galore, most of them involving music, dancing and lots of sex.

"Tonight is the winter solstice. This festival allows us to express our gratitude for the return of longer days. It is not a festival that celebrates the miracle of life, conception and growth as does the summer solstice."

I looked around at the lithe shapes clad in darker shades than I was used to seeing on the fae. Elle looked perfect in her blue gown, but even if she'd worn black she'd shine brighter than all the others put together.

"Figures you'd invite me to the dull party," I teased, relieved to see her perfect mouth curling up at the corners. "And I'm a vampire. Longer nights are more up my alley."

"This is the longest of them all, the perfect night to be a vampire."

"The perfect night to share with a lady of Faerie." She blushed and turned away, her sweet scent filling my body with desire. Afraid I'd made her nervous, I changed the subject. "So, are we in Faerie?" Other than the flowers it looked pretty much like a normal forest clearing.

"No, this is still your world." She gestured toward a group busily adding branches to the bonfire. "Although they live in Faerie as do most fae, these fae are not subjects of King Finvarra. This cluster of woodland fae are his allies, free spirits who honor the forests and the natural creatures who live there. They celebrate the festival here first, in Faerie later, hoping the Balance remains strong in both realms. She frowned suddenly and whispered, "Do not mention the murder of your tree."

"Ah. Got it." The bonfire was crackling, throwing lots of heat our way. "They're burning wood. That can't be too forest-friendly. Do they have to worry about the woodland police showing up?"

She rolled her eyes, a surprising thing for a fae to do. She must have learned it from Garrett's wife, Jackie. She and Elle liked to hang out together during the day. "They are burning branches that have already fallen. Dead wood."

"Good thing. Didn't want to get arrested at my first solstice."

I took in a deep breath, automatically checking for any species other than fae. If these woods were in the human realm, there was always a chance that a rogue werewolf could come barging in. As Garrett's second in command, it was part of my job description to always be on the alert for trouble.

She shook her head. "We are protected by the forest. No one else will enter."

If anyone else had breached my shields and read my mind I would have freaked, but this was Elle, and she already held my heart in her graceful hands, even though she hadn't a clue. I took another deep breath. "The fire has an odd smell." I wrinkled my nose, trying to distinguish the various layers of scent.

"The wood is birch and elder, signifying new beginnings. Various herbs are also added to promote the health of the forest habitat."

"Looks pretty healthy already." Besides the lush vegetation, the fae themselves seemed full of life. Although they were dressed in darker shades, these fae seemed more joyful than the fae I'd come in contact with, dancing around as they fed the bonfire, singing as they prepared their feast. There was nothing joyful about most of the residents of the Cascade Sidhe, the fae group I was used to dealing with, although Farrell and Brina had their fun moments.

"They're going to allow me to watch?" I asked, beginning to get excited. I'd never be invited to a Cascade solstice ceremony, so this might be my only chance to participate in one.

"You are my guest. Their only request is that you abide by their customs."

"I can do that." I mean how crazy could those customs be?

There was a mischievous glint in her eye. "Please remove your shoes and socks."

I glared at the sharp looking needles and jagged pieces of pine cones on the ground. "Um…"

"Trust me."

We removed our shoes and socks, my eyes shooting open as I noticed for the first time how lovely her feet were. She saw me looking and curled up her toes.

"What? Is it improper to admire a female's feet?" I asked.

"No, but you were looking at them with hunger in your eyes."

"I promise on my honor I would only *kiss* a lady's feet, no biting, unless she begged." I winked.

She stared at me like a rabbit under the gun, her fingers twisting around a lock of her long hair—a sweet habit she fell into when she was nervous. When she finally spoke I was floored. "That lady would be most fortunate."

Before I could respond, she turned, walking barefoot toward the bonfire at a fast pace. Once there she greeted a few of the woodland fae with polite nods, leaving me alone and stunned into silence. She'd actually flirted back. "Are you coming?" she asked, turning in place, her expression butter-melting.

I'm hopeful, Lady Elle.

"Right behind you," I called out, wincing again at my decision to wear such tight jeans. It was going to be a long night.

The ground felt nothing like what I'd imagined, as soft as my favorite slippers, but I wasn't wasting time thinking about my feet when the female of my dreams was giving me the green light.

4

ELLE

Had I gone too far? Misread his intentions? He had used his usual teasing tone, then added a phrase that left desire pooling in my belly. *"No biting, unless she begged."* Would he bite me if I begged, or would he turn away, disgusted by my audacity?

Perhaps we could enjoy each other this one night, the longest night of the year. And I would hold the sweet memory of our time together in my heart, warming me in the months and years to come. I knew he lusted for me, but that was nothing unusual for a vampire, a creature said to have a powerful sex drive. Jacqueline had told me when a vampire fed from a donor they often had sex.

To Sasha, I would simply be one more female he enjoyed, but for me it would be different. I wanted him enough to swallow my fear and give him pleasure, finding pleasure of my own in the strength of his body and the tenderness of his touch. He was kind and honest. He deserved my gift, even if it was only this once.

His hand rested on my lower back as we stood close to the bonfire. I relaxed and did not move away, enjoying the way his possessiveness made me almost feel worthy to be seen at his side. "You look lovely tonight, Elle." Long fingers traced the line of my jaw, knuckles skimmed my cheek, as if there was true feeling behind his gentleness.

I leaned against his hand, wanting more. "Thank you." I didn't tell him I'd agonized over choosing my gown, fixing my hair, even adding a touch of magic to make my cheeks a little rosy. Shameful, but I would not feel guilty that his compliment made my toes curl and my body ache.

Sasha moved his long hand up my arm, pulling me a tiny bit closer, but never so hard as to make me feel trapped. He understood my fears. I wanted to cry, my yearning for him was so great, but I would not act like a silly maiden. I would speak honestly, leaving the choice up to him.

The woodland fae had begun to chant in the language of my people, moving around the bonfire, throwing tiny sticks into the flames. They quickly caught fire and turned to ash, the thrower watching the color of the flames closely.

"What are they saying?" Sasha asked.

"Each petitioner thanks the forest and asks a personal boon. One might wish to leave behind some hurt, forget the memory so it does not affect their future, or one might ask to be shown the correct path to take toward love or happiness. Legend says that if the flame flares blue, the wish will come true.

He bent and handed me a stick, taking one for himself. "What will you wish for?"

"We may not speak it to each other in front of the fire. It is something we ask of the forest only."

Sasha faced the bonfire, speaking his request in Russian, tossing the stick into the flames. As he watched it burn, his pale skin was lit with the oranges and reds of the fire, giving him a dangerous glow. He was so handsome in that moment I could not breathe.

"Your turn." He grinned, not understanding how his closeness affected me. If he did, he would prove to be a most intelligent male by walking away and never looking back. I hoped perhaps he would not be so smart tonight.

"What's wrong, lovely lady? I thought the solstice ceremony was a happy time." He'd caught me lost in thought.

"You are right. I am being foolish." I turned and tossed my stick into the fire, asking for something I would never speak out loud.

"Are there other traditions?" He tucked a messy clump of hair behind my ear, his fingers playing with the arch, the lobe, his face leaning closer to kiss a sensitive spot below it. He stayed there breathing deeply of my scent, his hands stroking down my bare arms to weave between my fingers.

"There are bells, food, songs and dancing," I whispered into his fragrant hair. He smelled of the woods and the fire now, but his own scent, his maleness, always surrounded him. I wanted to bath in it.

He stepped back holding both of my hands in his. "Will you dance with me, Lady Elle, although I am only a simple dungeon dweller?" His wide smile urged me forward as he walked backward, tugging me along.

I pictured us together, our bodies moving in time with the traditional tunes and suddenly flashed on another vision. "If you dance with any other female, I will force you to wash your own dishes."

His eyes glinted with impish amusement. "You do know Rick and I purchased a modern miracle called a dishwasher, don't you?"

"Hmph. It is a waste of power." I glanced around at the other fae who'd begun dancing, realizing how selfish I'd sounded. "I am sure there are other females at the celebration that would appeal to you. I cannot be greedy."

He surprised me by stepping closer. "I see only you. No other female exists for me."

If only that were true. "I've been told you are a master of seduction, a wordsmith who teases and taunts a female into his bed. A male who wins his prize with kisses and caresses, then looks elsewhere."

"All true, I'm afraid." Against the light blue backdrop of his eyes, emotions flashed: yearning, sadness and resignation. But wasn't a warrior usually proud of his conquests?

"Unless two lovers are bound—meant to be together for life—it is normal to enjoy many." I stroked his face. "I trust you, Sasha, as I have not trusted for a long time. You would never be cruel." Courage filled my heart. "I have decided…"

Music drifted through the woods, an upbeat tune that interrupted my confession. Couples had already formed and were moving to the ancient rhythms and tunes played on musical instruments not often seen in this realm.

His grin grew wide again, his enthusiasm catching. "Dance with me, Elle, and I'll tell you what I wished for." He pulled me into the circle, laughing as he tried to copy what the others were doing.

We danced for hours—the brush of his body against mine sometimes a horrible torture and other times an unimagined joy. This tall vampire who'd thrown himself into the celebration as if he were a young fae, fascinated the free-spirited woodland elves. They offered him wine and shouted out encouragement. He learned the dance steps quickly, laughed with ease and tried to sing along with the traditional songs even though he did not know the language. During the feast, he watched me eat, sometimes insisting on feeding me morsels by hand. Being vampire, he could not eat, but the amount of honey wine he drank most certainly contributed to his joyful mood.

At one point he broke into a Russian ballad, surprising us with his clear, deep voice. He told us it was a sad tale of a human male, lost in the snowdrifts of the steppes, the blizzard a constant companion on the windblown, never ending plains. He was pining for his lover, speaking of the things he remembered in his last moments before death took him. The lovely way her hair spread out on the pillow when she looked up into his eyes, the way she kissed him, with her eyes open so she wouldn't miss a moment of their life together. After he'd translated the lyrics for me, I translated for the others. The words and melody were sad, the audience and the forest silent but for Sasha's strong voice.

Our fae hosts bowed to him at the end of the song, showing him great respect for honoring them and the forest with the gift of his music. He returned their bow, thanking them for allowing him to attend their ceremony. He was invited to return the following year.

And I was more in love with him than ever.

5

SASHA

I couldn't take my eyes off Elle the whole night. The way her hips swayed when she circled me in the dance, the way the fabric of her gown clung to her breasts, her nipples poking out at me as if to say, "Taste us." Thank god I'd worn a button down shirt, because untucked, it was just managing to hide my very painful erection.

When she allowed me to feed her by hand, her lips sucking on my fingers, I was so close to coming I had to make some excuse to walk around for several minutes, forcing the blood back where it belonged. She was the sexiest female I'd ever known, but that wasn't why I wanted her, at least not the only reason.

When I was with her, I could breathe. I forgot about all the shit from my past, the loss of my family, the unforgiveable things I'd been forced to do as a soldier and as a vampire in Eleanor's nest. When Garrett defeated our maker and saved my life by allowing me into his nest, I fought hard to gain the trust of the people I respected, putting my energy into finally doing some good in the world. It would never make up for the rest, but at least I could sleep most nights.

These last months with Elle had given me hope that I might have found a female who could forgive my past and share my future. She'd already healed me with her laughter as well as tortured me with her off-limits body for six months. She'd even put up with my constant teasing. Surely we were meant for each other.

And tonight she seemed to want more. She hadn't moved away when we'd danced close enough for her to feel my desire and she'd returned each of my lust filled gazes with heat in her eyes. It had taken a supreme effort not to drag her into the forest and tear off her gown, but I wouldn't take what wasn't clearly offered. She'd had to deal with years of that kind of degradation, but never from me.

No matter what happened between us, I would protect her for the rest of my days.

She was standing near the bonfire once more. "Elle..." She smiled at me full out, genuinely happy, a rarity for this fragile soul. "You having fun?" I took her hand and twisted her around in a spin.

She giggled, and the forest seemed to take the lovely sound and send it echoing through its branches. Now all the fae were smiling at us. "Yes. It's lovely here. I forget..." And so quickly her smile was gone.

I frowned in frustration. "Tell me what I can do to make you smile again."

Golden fire burned in her violet eyes as she ran her hands firmly up my chest to clutch at my shirt. "Will you stay and share the rest of this night with me?"

"Of course. I said I would." I touched her nose with the tip of my index finger, trailing my finger over her plump lips and strong chin, adding another to trace the lines of her long neck. My gaze stilled on her pulse.

I hadn't fed tonight.

"Then I wish for you to kiss me." She lifted her chin, opening her mouth, the tip of her tongue wetting the corner.

The erotic offering stole my breath, shot fire to my groin and blood to my cock. It was more than a kiss she wanted. I leaned down and brushed her lips with mine, the taste of her exquisite: all spices and honey wine.

She held me by the collar, her hands in tight fists, trembling. "Again."

Again was what I wanted too, only slow and careful, staying in control. Never frightening her. I just wasn't sure I could pull it off. I wanted her so much my need had become a beast inside me. And a beast inside a hungry vampire could be lethal.

She began to turn away, perhaps thinking my hesitation meant I'd rejected her. I leaned closer and clasped her shoulders, my forehead against hers. "I've wanted you for a long time. I don't know if I can be gentle."

"I do not expect nor wish you to be gentle, my warrior." She released her grip on my shirt and led me to an oak tree, out of the line of sight of the still-celebrating fae. She leaned against it, smiling. "Kiss me again."

This time, an order. Elle the warrior had made her appearance and it turned me on more than her meek submission ever would. Tonight I would be at her mercy, I would worship her body, I would give her control. But so far, she'd spoken of kisses, nothing else, so kisses it was. To prevent my hips from grinding against hers, I kept my feet back and spread apart, my palms flat against the enormous trunk and bracketing her face.

Impatient, she tugged on my hair. "Sasha..."

But before she could speak the rest, I covered her mouth —our tongues and lips exploring with delight. I embraced the moan that erupted from my chest when the full taste of her exploded in my mouth. She was perfection. Honey sweet and pepper hot. We feasted on each other until she had to break away for breath.

She'd echoed my noises with sweet ones of her own, grabbing hold of my waistband and yanking my hips forward. I yielded, taking it slow no longer an option. She was almost as tall as I was and the perfect positioning, my cock brushing against her center, hadn't helped my attempt to stay in control.

I buried my nose in her hair. "Elle," I whispered. "If you're not ready..."

"Am I behaving as if that were the case?" She snapped, biting my bottom lip and pulling on it with her teeth, drawing blood. She scraped her tongue along one of my fangs and I tasted something sweet and salty and incredible.

Uh—not good. Maybe she didn't get that I was a very hungry vampire. It had been dumbass stupid of me not to feed before we left the house. The scent of her blood was overpowering my restraint and the way she was wiggling against me, sure wasn't helping.

"Touch me," she whispered, nibbling on my ear lobe.

I thought about it for two seconds. Maybe three. "I'm going to take you against this tree, if you don't stop wiggling."

"I want that."

Who was I to argue with a fae lady? My hand slid down to cup her breast, the soft fabric of her dress offering no barrier. Her nipple peaked and I rolled and pinched it until she moaned and sighed, still wiggling against my cock. I'd used my other hand to hike up her dress, and I let out my own moan when I felt how wet she was.

"Sasha..."

"I'm here, love." I kissed her hard.

My fingers brushed her sex, sliding inside and teasing her clitoris. Her scent was heaven and the changing expressions on her lovely face as I brought her closer to orgasm altered my world. Bringing her pleasure, protecting her, loving her, this was all I wanted in life.

She arched against me when she came, crying out softly, her knees giving out. I helped her to the ground and we sat side by side, out backs against the enormous trunk. I stoked her hair and kissed her palms. "You are so beautiful. Sometimes I can't think when I look at you."

She smiled, her eyes still glazed over with pleasure. "Give me this one night, Sasha, and I will ask for nothing else from you."

I straightened up, leaning away. "What did you say?" I must have misheard her.

"You know I'm not worthy to be the lover of an honorable male. I only ask for this one night of passion so that I might remember—"

I stood and offered her my hand. "We're going home. Put on your shoes."

"What did I say?" She followed me to the edge of the clearing, clutching at her skirt.

I spun to face her. "Do you think I'm like those fae lords who used you and hurt you? The ones who've made you cry for months?"

"No, of course not."

"It doesn't sound that way."

"I'm giving myself to you. You are not forcing me or using me."

"I'm not interested in only one night with you. I thought you got that."

"Then a week. A month. I will obey your wishes."

She was looking down at the ground, completely submissive like she must have been with those other males. I grabbed her by the shoulders, feeling my eyes turn silver in anger, my fangs extend. "And then what? You'll hop into bed with someone else?"

"Sasha—"

She was trembling. I was scaring her. *Shit.*

"I'm sorry." I released her and searched for my shoes. I'm going for a walk. I need to calm down. I'll be back, and then we'll talk."

"Wait. The time!"

Using vamp speed, I slipped on my shoes and socks, then raced down the path we'd used to get here, putting as much distance as I could between me and the most frustrating female in California. Because I hadn't fed, my speed petered out pretty fast. As I panted, leaning against a tree to support myself, I looked down for the first time. The snow was melting, soaking through my boots. Dreading what I'd find, I looked up. There was a glow on the top leaves of the oak grove.

The sun.

6

ELLE

I paced near the path he'd taken. He did not realize the danger he was in. The woodland fae had spelled this clearing to make the night last longer, but it was dawn in his world. I'd sometimes seen him out in the sun but I understood that he could not remain exposed to its rays for long. Perhaps thirty minutes, no more.

And he had not fed from me, leaving him weakened.

This was my fault. I'd treated him without respect, never imagining he might have genuine, loving feelings toward me. My heart had been shocked to hear him say it wasn't only lust that drew his gaze to my body. My dream had come true and I had tossed it aside with a stupid remark.

Now it was my duty to protect him, to save him from his foolish mistake. Could I muster up the strength, the courage to use the lines? I was so afraid to try, but now I had no choice, even if it drained me to exhaustion. Even if King Finvarra sensed my presence and called me back to court, perhaps forcing me to take up my old life. Only Sasha mattered.

Before I had a chance to change my mind, I threw myself into the magic of Faerie—the heat, the energy, the music of the ley lines, as familiar to me as my own heartbeat. I stretched out my magical tendrils in the direction Sasha had run, remembering the way his lips had felt on mine, the way his fingers had moved inside me, the way he'd given and not taken. Listening for the music of his energy, I focused on only him.

I stumbled into a grove of oak trees, discovering him crawling toward a thick patch of shrubs. I ran to him. "Get up. You must rise, now."

"I can't." His exposed skin was beginning to redden and blister.

"You must. There is a place nearby where you will be safe."

He struggled to his feet, draping an arm over my shoulder. His skin felt so hot. "How did you...find me?" he said, the hoarseness of his voice the opposite of his usual rich tones.

The answer was surprising, even to me, but also true. "We are connected, heart to heart."

"My heart's been...dead for...a long time," He grunted, the pain getting worse.

"I am not referring to the organ." I pulled him along a little faster, although my strength was not what it should have been.

"You took the lines?" I nodded. "Get us...home?"

"No. It has weakened me. Why did you not call Garrett? He can tolerate the sun for much longer periods. He and Jacqueline can travel the lines."

"They are...in France for two weeks." Sasha was shivering.

"There, you see?" I pointed toward a dark and seemingly damp cave, full of who knew what—hopefully, not a hibernating bear or a nest of snakes. I helped him crawl as far inside as possible, then as he panted on his hands and knees, I ran out to find some dry leafy branches to use as a bed. I spread them out and after a few more trips had him lie down on top of them, hoping he would stay dry. The cave was cold and smelled of rotting plants, but it was a haven nonetheless.

He was trembling with cold, face down on the makeshift bed. To warm him I covered him with my shawl, wrapping it gently around his arms and shoulders. Now that he was out of the sun, his wounds had begun to heal, but he was still so weak. "Sasha, let me feed you."

"Elle, no..."

"Shh." I rubbed his neck and kissed his shoulder. "You need blood."

"My control isn't what it should be."

"You won't hurt me." I moved away and assisted him in rolling over, both of us wincing when he groaned in pain. "My brave warrior." I kissed his lips, but when his fangs extended, he pushed me away.

"Too close to the pointy bits." He was able to laugh, a sure sign of his recovery, albeit not fast enough to suit me. "It was a dumbass move to leave before I asked about the time difference. I've heard what can happen with fae magic and I should have thought..."

A stray lock of hair covered one of his eyes. I brushed it to the side so I might see both. "I should have warned you." I lifted his hand and kissed his palm. "I confess that I have watched you train. At the risk of causing your ego to swell, I know you to be a strong warrior."

He clutched at his stomach. The healing process was stealing his reserves. "It's best...if you go to get help," he said through gritted teeth. "I'll be fine now that I'm out of the sun."

I sat up and spoke more assertively. "I see you are in pain. You will stop being stubborn and take my blood. Arguing with me is fruitless."

He tried to smile, but the pain was too great. "You don't understand. I may not be able to stop. I'd never hurt you on purpose, but I—"

"Then I will beg you to bite me." His eyes widened. "You said you would bite a female if she begged you. Is that not true?"

A crease formed between his eyes. "I believe...we were discussing feet."

"Blood from my wrist will taste better and the bite will be less painful."

"And you know this, how?" He'd managed to get himself up on his elbows.

I tilted my head in thought. "Garrett drank from my wrist when I offered to share with him. He was weak and in great need. No one has taken blood from my feet so I do not know for certain if it would be less pleasant, but I would imagine it is so."

Despite his pain, he smiled widely. "Do you know where it tastes the best?" He looked me over from head to...

"You are a rogue with a dirty mind." But his words made my body sing with heat, imagining his mouth in that intimate, needy spot. I ached for him so. I placed my hand on his chest, where his heart used to beat. "You need the strength my blood will bring you."

He grasped my hand and held it there. "I need you, Elle,

not your magic. I look into your eyes and I'm lost. I'm never happier than when we're together, even those few times you've been angry with me."

I smiled and placed his hand on my chest. My heart was beating faster than I could ever remember. "I want to share my blood with you. You will not hurt me."

He winced as another wave of pain swept through him. "I'm dying, yet all I can think about is making love to you, even if it's the last thing I do."

"I will not allow it to be the last thing you do. Feed from me, Sasha, and as you drink I will tell you what I wished for at the bonfire." I would open my heart to the male who'd stolen mine, even if he left me shattered.

"You're weak too."

"You must regain your strength. We have not finished." I slid my hand down his body and squeezed, enjoying the look of pleasure on his face.

He managed a laugh and gave in, accepting my wrist and biting down quickly, each swallow of my rich blood healing the remains of his burns and returning his strength. "Tell me," he mumbled, his lips brushing my palm before going back to his feeding.

I trembled and I knew he felt it even in my wrist. He lifted his gaze. "I wished to spend the entire night in the arms of the vampire warrior with whom I have fallen in love." I combed through his blonde hair with my fingers. He closed his eyes and moaned. "I wished to bring him pleasure and heal a small bit of the pain I sometimes see reflected in his eyes."

Sasha licked my small wound, then pulled me toward him, kissing me firmly on the mouth. When he finished, he grinned, teasing, "I'll kill that guy whoever he is." I smacked his stomach and he grunted, pretending to be in pain. "It's you, silly vampire."

"But you must know, don't you? Every minute I spend with you heals me." He cradled my face between his large hands. "Tell me the truth. Do you really only want one night?"

I crawled closer, relieved his skin had healed and joyful I'd assisted in his recovery. I rested my hand on his chest moving it in a slow circle. Even without a beating heart, he could not be more alive to me than he was at this moment. I kept my eyes turned down, afraid to see his expression when I confessed. "I would ask for a lifetime, but I do not have the right."

He lifted my chin. "Elle. Hear me, please. You weren't responsible for what Fionna allowed those males to do to you. You fought against them with every ounce of your energy."

"I tried, but I was too weak. The things they made me do…" I shuddered and turned away. "I am unfit to stand beside you."

"Shush. You're the most perfect female ever created. A lifetime with you won't be long enough." He kissed my eyes, my cheeks, my mouth—our passion growing once more.

"Can you look at me and not see…not see…"

"I see my Lady Elle, a warrior who not only survived, but triumphed. I would be honored if you stood beside me, although I like this position even better." Our next kiss was deeper, more demanding, his tongue dancing with mine in the most delicious way. When he moved away, Sasha's expression held a note of yearning. "I've done horrible things in my past. I still kill when it's necessary. You may not want to stick around when you hear the details."

His hand had moved to my ankle, beginning to slowly push up the hem of my gown. He was giving me the time to say no and I had no doubt he would stop if I asked him to. Those other males had laughed when I'd begged. "Death is sometimes required to sustain balance." I visualized gutting them all, especially Kennet and Fionna.

"When I was in the tsar's army, I helped to burn villages. The people did not escape. Not even the children."

His eyes glistened with the guilt he still carried. I cradled his face and he placed his hands over mine, as if he couldn't bear to release them. "The Sasha I know is honorable and compassionate. This male would no longer follow orders that destroyed innocent lives. We will leave our pasts where they cannot hurt us and look to our future together." Not able to resist a moment longer, I stood, unfastening my gown and allowing it to pool at my feet. I was naked, displayed for his eyes alone. "May I have my wish?"

"Only if you wish for a lifetime instead of a day." He drank me in with his eyes, resting on certain places longer than others. My face heated in a way I hadn't experienced since I was a maiden.

"I freely give myself to you tonight and every night to come."

I was on my back and underneath him in seconds, his clothes in a pile beside my gown. He clasped my hands, pulling them over my head and holding them there. I'd been restrained with ropes and chains many times by many different males. Torture would usually follow. But Sasha was my love, my heart, and I knew to the depths of my soul he would never hurt me. In fact the inability to move beneath him accentuated my need.

"Lady Elle, you—are—mine. " He spoke with a fierceness I did not recognize. "No other male will ever touch you or hurt you, because I'll kill them if they do." He kissed me to seal his promise, rough and possessive, a marking of his territory. His tongue stroked over mine, his fangs scraping my lips, nibbling and drawing a drop or two of blood. "I can't wait to taste you everywhere."

It occurred to me that before we went any farther I should stake my claim as well. "I will kill any female who touches you."

He shrugged. "I'll need to feed almost every day. I'll make sure it isn't an erotic experience for my donors."

I rolled suddenly, flipping him over and straddling his hips. "You will feed from only me. I do not weaken as a mere human does."

"Sometimes I go on assignment and am away from the house for several weeks."

"Then I will join you. You will teach me to fight with a sword or a knife as you do."

He laughed at my wild command. "Yes, Lady Elle. I have no doubt you will become my favorite pupil. But there still may be times..."

I narrowed my eyes and kissed him again, marking my own territory with hungry lips. I frowned. "You have not told me what you wished for at the bonfire, even though I kept my word and danced with you until I was dizzy."

"You're beautiful when you're dizzy." Sasha stroked my face, my shoulder, my breasts. I arched into his hands, cherishing his touch, so different from the touch of any other. His heated expression warmed my belly and I ached for him to join his body to mine.

He laid his hand over my heart, the way I had his. "I wished I could be a male you trusted with your heart and your body. A male worthy of speaking your full name."

I couldn't breathe for a moment, the truth of his words

almost too much to take in. Sasha wanted my love, my respect, my trust, not knowing he had them already. My last defenses fell, crumbling to dust. "A mate?"

"Your mate."

I lifted my body and slid down his sex, opening my mind and senses as we became one. When he was fully seated, I explored his chest and shoulders and arms with my hands and mouth.

"Elle..." he whispered reverently as he brushed his thumbs against my already erect nipples. I arched my back as he rose up to put his mouth on me, the lightning shooting from each nipple to my sex, adding more slickness to my wet channel. Sasha's light blue eyes had glazed over in pleasure, yet he held himself still inside me, weaving his fingers in my hair, forcing my mouth to meet his in a passionate exchange.

When we broke apart we touched forehead to forehead, sharing breaths and heated gazes. "My gentle warrior. I was called Eleandra as a child. It is a name worthy of a lady of Faerie."

His wide smile warmed my soul. "I love you, Eleandra."

My smile returned the love of this male who knew my secrets but did not allow them to brand me. "I trust you with my heart, my soul, Sasha Vodinski, and I will love you for all time. I swear this on the longest night of the year, a sacred time for our people." He flipped me onto my back, taking my hands and stretching them over my head once more. "You wish to take charge, my warrior?" I tried to wiggle beneath him but he had me trapped.

"I've waited for ages to have you beneath me. We have all day, and I'm going to take my time."

"You are certainly a male of infinite patience, but there is just one more thing."

"Oh?" He ground his hips into mine then stopped again. He was obviously resolved to drive me crazy.

"Next year you will bring a live tree into your home and we will replant it in the forest. Sinlae does not need more compost."

He grinned. "Anything. It's your house now, too."

To have a true home again, a family, was more than I had ever imagined. "Then today I am your slave," I teased.

I gasped when he bit into my ear lobe, sucking the drops that formed. In retaliation I squeezed my inner muscles so hard he growled and finally began to move, stroking in and out slowly at first, creating a friction that would bring me to orgasm all too soon. He filled me in the most exquisite way.

I moaned and moved my hips in sync with his rhythm, wanting so much to touch him, yet forced to submit. When I reached the edge I opened my body and mind to the release, allowing it to take me into a pleasure so strong I cried out in surprise and elation. He released my hands and moved faster, extending my pleasure and finding his own.

It took several moments to find our words. "You are exquisite, my love," he whispered, stroking my cheek.

I stretched and purred. "I feel loose limbed and impossibly randy."

"The first time is just the warm up."

"Set me on fire." I leaned closer and bit his shoulder, then grabbed a thick lock of his hair and pulled him closer.

When his fangs extended fully, he moved down my body to find the large vein in my inner thigh. By the time the sun set that evening, I was sore and satisfied and more in love with my warrior than ever. We traveled the lines to his bedroom and slept for many hours wrapped in each other's arms. I had given up hope of finding such happiness, never imagining a vampire warrior with a troubled soul would bring magic as strong as any fae to rekindle my damaged heart. I'd found a home, a family with Sasha and the Rogues, a reason to live again.

I snuggled closer, hoping he'd awaken soon.

7

SASHA

I t was Christmas Eve and the party was in full swing. Rick and Liam had outdone themselves cooking and ordering the most delicious food, and I'd made sure the bar was well stocked. We had a small band playing in the corner and everyone was dancing, eating, drinking or kissing under the mistletoe.

"What is this?" Eleandra held up a candy cane, sniffing it suspiciously.

"It's a magical treat called a candy cane."

"Oh? Magical in what way? I do not sense power emanating from it. I smell mint, but that is a most ordinary fragrance."

"Except at Christmastime. Mint symbolizes the fae and the red symbolizes the blood they share with their vampire mates."

She giggled, something she'd been doing more and more lately. "And it is bent in such a way because?"

"So her mate can hook her by the wrist and bring her under the mistletoe for a kiss, or a bite." I used the end of the candy cane to illustrate my story.

"Her mate." She'd whispered the word like a benediction.

"For all time, remember?"

A male's rich voice interrupted. "Only if I approve her choice."

Even though I'd never met the guy, I knew who he was by the expression on my future mate's face. Finvarra, the King of Faerie, stood beside me, wearing the same arrogant glare his grandson, Aedus, often used to bully those who didn't agree with him. I placed myself between Elle and her king, meeting his gaze with my own brand of power.

The music had stopped and everyone but Elle, the king and I were frozen in place. I'd forgotten Finvarra's magic was strong enough to stop time and seeing it happen before my eyes was shattering. I swallowed down the small amount of spit still in my mouth, stretching out my hand to Eleandra, who was already kneeling before her king. "You're mine. You don't have to kneel to this guy anymore."

"He is my sovereign lord. If he commands me to return to Faerie, I must go."

"Over my dead body." I spun to face this so-called ruler. "You allowed your people to torture her. She's not going back with you."

He grinned in an incredibly annoying way. "They are no longer my people. Every one who hurt her or any of the others has been...dispatched."

"Too late."

"Yes, I agree." The king stretched out his own hand and Elle grasped it. "Rise, my sweet and let me look at you."

"Yes, lord."

He scanned her, then me with black eyes that spoke of untold centuries. "Is the vampire good to you?"

"He is the very best male imaginable."

That comment produced a smile. "Truly? And you wish to be his lifemate?"

"I do."

He turned to me, grasping my forearm and breaking through my shields as if they were nonexistent. "And will you protect her with your life, your blood, your strength, your honor?"

It was hopeless to battle against this ancient creature, although I would never show weakness. "I will, not that it's any of your business."

"Even against me?"

"Especially against you."

"I could rip off your head before you take your next breath."

"You could try."

And Fin laughed, releasing my arm and looking around the room for the first time. "What is this celebration?"

I took a couple of breaths to calm myself down, then answered. "A human holiday."

"May I stay? It seems a pleasant gathering."

"Depends," I muttered.

He lifted Elle's chin and kissed both of her cheeks. "Do you think I would deny the happiness of a child who has suffered so under my daughter's rule? As long as she lives in this realm, I grant her the freedom to make her own choices. I only ask two things. That she comes when Faerie has need of her magic and also to keep her body and mind healthy and strong. All creatures with fae blood must spend time in their own realm on a regular basis. You may accompany her."

"Gee. Thanks."

"I also insist that I be allowed to visit her here on occasion. I am often at Jacqueline and Garrett's home, or Liam's.

"Why would Faerie need her magic?"

"Surely you know we are on the brink of war."

"She won't be going to war without me by her side." We stared at each other. He nodded.

"Is all of that okay with you?" I asked Eleandra, halfway hoping she'd throw the dude out on his ear.

"I will serve my people with pride and would be most honored, sire, if you would come to see us in our home." Elle was beaming, making me feel guilty for not thinking about her happiness. If her king respected her enough to be a guest in her home, no one in Faerie would be allowed to treat her poorly. A clever move. Maybe this guy wasn't so bad after all.

Finvarra's ear-to-ear grin was catching. He must have some of that charisma magic. "Excellent." He snapped his fingers and the party was suddenly back in full swing. "Do you have honey wine?"

"Yes. At the bar." I pointed in that direction.

"We must toast your happiness tonight."

"Thank you." Why did I get the feeling he intended to drink me under the table?

He waved at Liam's partner. "Kellaine, grandchild, come and dance with your king." And he was off, singing and dancing, eating and drinking along with the rest of the crew. Weird how he fit right in.

"Sasha." My glorious female nuzzled my neck, an incredibly hot sensation.

"Yes, Eleandra?"

"We are under the mistletoe, and I've hooked you with my candy cane." She'd hooked it in my hair—leaving it dangling there.

"I think this calls for a kiss."

"And a bite?"

"Whatever my lady requires."

I HOPE you enjoyed Winter Solstice Wishes. If you'd like to know more about Sasha, Elle, and the rest of the Rogues Team, the best place to start would be with *Rebirth* - Rogues Shifter Series Book One by Gayle Parness. *Rebirth* in ebook form is permanently free at all vendors.

https://books2read.com/Rebirth-Rogues-Shifter

To learn more about my books check out my website.

https://www.gayleparness.com

I've included an excerpt from my first Rogues Inc. novella on the next page. *A Stubborn Heart* involves a witch who needs help to find her daughter and a cougar shifter, who wants nothing more than to be left alone.

A STUBBORN HEART EXCERPT

BY GAYLE PARNESS

A Stubborn Heart is book one in the Rogues Inc. Series. It involves one of the original Rogues Inc. team members - Sinclair - and the werewolf - Gabriel - who stole her heart when she was a teen and living with his pack. They'd been apart for many years when a tragedy threw them together once more.

Chapter One

"Sinc, no!"

I was already on the porch with my hand on the door-knob. Leaving without my phone was not an option. Kyle would probably text me with questions about the lab work and I had to be available.

I opened the door and moved into the house.

Something huge slammed into my body, sharp and hot and horribly loud, throwing me across the floor and into the wall. My ears thrummed for a moment before all sounds abandoned me. Blood scent. Burning. Darkness.

～

Dreams.

Whispers. "…bomb…"

Knives pricking.

Burned flesh.

Hurt to breathe.

Let me sleep.

Cold. So cold.

A hundred knives.

Please, please.

Let me sleep.

Bomb?

I tried to swallow, but no saliva. With a huge effort, I spread my fingers. A blanket. A bed. But no sounds. Dead ears.

Opening my eyes, I saw doctors and nurses talking, talking, talking, but not speaking to *me*. Look at me! I lifted my hand to pound on the bed, but it didn't obey my orders.

So tired.

I was in the hospital. That was good. I guess. A muffled sound shocked me. The scent of eucalyptus. Ethan, leaning over and talking next to my ear.

"…okay. You'll be okay."

Were we underwater? Hard to understand.

He moved away and smiled, his eyes brightening when he saw I was looking at him. He moved his mouth. I clasped his shirt to pull him closer. Couldn't hear.

"*Ethan. What happened?*" I thought the words, but we couldn't mind speak. He didn't hear me.

A nurse appeared. Drowsy now. No pain. Blessed sleep.

My lids were manhole covers, too heavy to lift without tools.

"Open your eyes. For me. Try hard."

Ethan stood beside me clutching my hand, doctors at the end of the bed. "Sinc. You're going...okay," Ethan said.

I could make out some words. "Ringing, but I can hear you now. Mostly. I was deaf."

A doctor nodded. "Excellent. We'll have your ears tested soon."

What did he mean, excellent? Nothing was excellent. A damn truck had run me down. Only... It wasn't a truck. I was... I was in the house. The one we'd used while we were investigating the disappearance of those boys at my old pack in Los Altos. What the hell had happened?

Ethan tugged on my hand so I'd look at him. "Sinc, honey." Ethan looked as if he'd lost his best friend. "Your foot is badly injured."

"What? My foot?" My words were starting to slur. Couldn't feel my body. Couldn't test my limits. Couldn't connect to my leopard. Shit. "Dizzy."

"They gave you pain meds. The doctors want to amputate to save the rest of your leg."

"Amulet?" I shook my head. "I can't think straight."

Kyle was suddenly leaning over me. I hadn't seen him before. He looked worried. I must be a mess. He spoke slowly. "Would you rather deal with the pain so your head clears?" I nodded and touched his familiar face. He grinned at me and moved away. "Stop the drip," he said to the doctors.

I glared at the group at the foot of my bed. One of them walked over to the tubes and made an adjustment. "I need to understand what happened," I tried to explain.

Ethan squeezed my hand. "It was a bomb."

"A bomb." I'd heard someone say that before. "The house?" He nodded. "A bomb went off in the house?"

"Yes."

"Oh god. Who else got hurt?"

"Brina, but she'll be okay. Jackie got cut up. Thank the gods the vampires were in Crescent City."

"Gabe?"

"It's his fault," Kyle snapped.

"His family placed the bomb in the basement. He says he knew about it, but they'd threatened to hurt his mom. He was trying to save you, but you turned around and ran back inside," Ethan said.

Kyle pushed Ethan out of the way. "You need surgery, but you don't have a lot of time to think about it."

Ethan glared at Kyle, who just shrugged and took a few steps back. Ethan continued. "What's left of your foot... It has to go. Too much energy is being channeled to an area that can't heal. If it's removed, the rest of your natural shifter healing will kick in."

"I can try to shift now."

"You don't have the energy. It will do more harm than good." One of the doctors had answered.

He was right. I couldn't even connect to my leopard. "So if I don't agree to the amputation, I'll lose my leg too?" Words were coming easier now.

"I'm sorry Ms. Blakefield." The doctor stepped around to the other side of the bed. "We'll have to amputate from the knee if you wait too long."

"Nice bedside manner." I grumbled, wincing as pain enveloped my body in a rush. The meds were wearing off. Big time. Shifters had super fast metabolisms. In this case it sucked.

Ethan looked like he was either going to grab my shoulders and shake me or pull me into a hug. "The team needs you. We all need you. Say yes."

I'd be a cripple. Useless in a fight. Yeah, the team would need me to sit at the computer and do my brilliant techy thing, but that wasn't what I'd trained for. I wanted out in the field. I wanted to fight our enemies the way the rest of them did. I wanted… I wanted…

Gabe's face flashed in my mind. He'd known about the bomb and had tried to save me, but he'd been willing to sacrifice the others.

I knew what I wanted. I wanted to face him again. To show him what he'd done. To make him hurt the way I did. I wanted to live. "Do it."

The doctor nodded and readjusted my drip. I was out before I had a chance to say goodbye to Ethan or Kyle.

Uhhh. Nausea. Pain. Open eyes. Too much light. Close eyes. More rest, please.

"Hey, sleepy." Ethan's voice. "You're gonna be okay."

"You keep saying that but it's still up for debate." I pushed away from my pillow. "Uch. I drooled."

"You've drooled before."

"Have not." A lie. He'd seen me drool. Ethan and I had been lovers until I'd messed it up. He was better off without me.

"I won't argue with a patient," he said, smiling.

"Is it the next day?"

Ethan looked at his phone. "Yeah, it's around nine in the morning."

"Where's Kyle?"

"Home with Peter."

The room was empty. "Great turnout. Guess you're my only friend."

"Plenty of people have peeked in."

"Uh huh."

"They're coming back. Look."

He indicated a table in the corner. It was covered with presents and flowers and balloon bouquets. What was up with balloon bouquets anyway? This wasn't a damn party. I'd lost my... "What's that?" I pointed toward a stuffed animal.

"A snow leopard from Jackie and Garrett."

I held out my hands.

He brought it over. It was soft and adorable. Huggable. I shifted in the bed to make room under the covers for the leopard, then glanced down the length of the bed. My legs were whole, my right foot completely under the blanket. The bandaged stump that used to have a foot attached to it was sticking out. I clutched the toy to my chest and stared at the ugly injury. "Cover it."

Ethan did what I asked without showing me an ounce of pity. Thank the gods for Ethan. "It doesn't matter. You're powerful and beautiful and irreplaceable on the team."

"Sure." My eyes burned.

"Hi!" Kyle's voice rang through the mostly empty room.

Visitors. Great. Now they show up.

Rob, Kyle and Peter were first, but didn't stay for long, taking my quiet mood as a sign I was tired or in pain. In mourning was more like it, but I wasn't about to discuss feelings I'd only just begun to deal with. Liam and Kaera showed up, and I was happy to see neither of them had been badly injured. It could have been so much worse. My friends did their best not to stare at the empty space at the bottom of the bed, but it was the snow leopard in the room—too large to ignore. Or maybe too absent to ignore.

Jackie arrived while I was eating the hospital's idea of lunch. Tasteless vegetable soup. "It took you long enough to get here. Everyone else has visited me. At least everyone I expect to visit." Jackie glanced at the IV bag before sitting in the chair beside my bed. "It's usually dispersing a pain killer," I explained. "Very nice, but it makes me sleepy. I knew you'd drag your ass here at some point, so now it's only dripping saline."

"How do you feel?"

"How do you think I feel knowing I'll never wear another pair of Jimmy Choos?" Sarcasm was my shield of choice.

"You could still wear one." Her smile was more concerned than happy.

"Yes, but I'd have to pay for two. It goes against my principles, or it would, if I had any principles."

Relief shone in her green eyes. My quips were doing their job. Jackie had enough cause for anxiety without me adding to the mix. "You have principles. You just try to keep them a secret from the rest of us."

"Ha. Glad to see my evil plan is working. But how are *you* feeling? And Brina? I heard she was hurt badly."

"Liam told me Brina will be as good as new in a week or so. And I've healed, thanks to my cheetah and a bit of blood from Garrett. He'll be coming when he wakes up from his rest."

"He doesn't have to. Not much to see here."

"He's been worried about you."

"Doc said his blood helped stop the bleeding. Might have saved me."

"You're a close friend. We'd do anything for you."

What a power couple those two had turned out to be. When Jackie, a cheetah shifter, was introduced as part of our new team of rogues, I thought she was just a pretty face who could run fast. Nothing special. She kicked my ass that first day, then quickly became my closest friend, surpassing all of us with her healer, cheetah and demon magic. Garrett had always been a powerful vampire, made more powerful by the fact he was born a cheetah shapeshifter before being turned against his will. The two of them together were practically unbeatable.

"So what's new?" I tried to sound nonchalant, but it was an epic fail.

"I've been entertaining a house guest."

"What are you planning on doing with Gabe?"

She hesitated. "We're having a team meeting tonight at the house." I frowned and glanced away. It was the first of many meetings I'd be missing. "I'll make sure you're kept in the loop. Kaera is coming. Aaron too. He'll know what to do about Gabe."

"I guess Garrett is pissed off at me, huh?" I coughed in an attempt to hide the catch in my voice.

"Why do you think that?"

"He put me in charge at the house. I should have known something was up when Gabe rushed me out."

"Kaera and I were there, we just weren't putting out feelers to see if he was lying. It was our responsibility as well as yours."

I sighed. "Thanks for trying."

"Gabe admitted to showing up only to save your life. He told us Karl threatened him with Katrina's death if he warned any of us. He figured he could get you out without repercussions." Jackie squeezed my hand. "When can you go home?"

"Tomorrow, I think." I was anxious to get out of here, but the prospect of moving in with Kyle was a little daunting.

"You'll stay with me. No arguing. I'll put you in my old room on the first floor."

"Are you sure, because Kyle offered, and he's been really sweet. I think he'd make a big effort not to annoy me, but Ethan is there and it would be awkward." Ethan and I were over, even though a part of me wished I could be the girl he needed me to be. He was the kind of mate most females dreamed of snatching up. A heart the size of Seattle, movie star good looks, and honest to a fault.

"You're family. We want you there."

I sighed. Jackie's offer meant more to me than I could put into words. I sat up a little straighter and met her worried gaze. "I could be dead, or badly burned, or worse. I have to keep telling myself that I'm lucky. I mean it sucks and I've cried and I'll probably keep crying, but I still have a job that I love and friends who have my back. And—and in a fight I can...can shoot a crossbow, I guess—if Garrett keeps me on the team."

My throat burned, my eyes filling with liquid. "I've already started looking into a prosthesis. Maybe Kyle and I can put our heads together to come up with something that'll work for a snow leopard." I looked down, surprised to see I was hugging the toy leopard tightly to my chest.

Jackie crawled onto the bed and put her arms around me. The dam broke as sniffles turned to sobs. "I'm—I'm sorry. I'm being such an...an idiot."

"We're all here for you. I believe in you, and so does everyone else. You'll kick the ass of this glitch and come back stronger than ever. It might take a little time, so be patient."

"Do you think I can? Come back strong?"

"Garrett said so himself."

A soothing warmth—like a cozy magical blanket—seeped into my muscles and bones. I gasped and pulled away, gazing at Jackie with wide eyes. "Holy shit." We both laughed at the shocked sound of my voice. "You gave me healing energy?" She smiled. "If you could bottle that magic, no one would need pain meds." This was the first time I'd had a chance to experience her healer gift first hand. I blew my nose with a tissue from a box she'd handed me. "Thanks, witchy woman."

"I wish I could have healed..." We looked at the end of the bed at the same time. "I wouldn't have known what to do."

"It's fine. I'm fine." I prayed she wouldn't feel the lie.

We spoke softly for a while longer, then Garrett arrived, smiling when he found us in the bed together.

"Is this one of your fantasies?" I teased him.

He laughed and hugged me. "Good to see your wit has returned full force."

"Garrett, I have to ask you—"

"You can start work again as soon as you feel you're ready. But there's no rush. And you're staying with us, correct? We can talk again when you're out of the hospital and more comfortable."

"You're not angry?"

"Certainly not at you."

"But you'd left me in charge."

"Jackie and Kaera's senses were tricked as well. We scanned the house early on and observed nothing other than the expected hidden microphones and cameras. Kyle is beating himself up over missing the hidden bomb, just as you are." Garrett squeezed my hand, smiling his reassurance. "No blame falls on your shoulders or any of our team.

This was the Los Altos Pack's doing, and rest assured, the ring leaders will be punished severely."

"Gabe?"

He and Jackie exchanged a look, both frowning. "Nothing's been decided yet," he said.

A Stubborn Heart is available at all vendors.
https://books2read.com/StubbornHeart

ALSO BY GAYLE PARNESS

Paranormal Romance & Paranormal Fantasy:

Rogues Shifter Series:

Rebirth (Free at all vendors)

Stalked

Twisted

Blown Away

Caught Between

Torn Apart

Cut Off

Blood Spelled

Book 9 coming in 2019

Triad Series: A spinoff involving one of the key characters from the Rogues Shifter Series

Breaking Out

Falling Out

Spinning Out

Rogues Inc. Series: Novella length

A Stubborn Heart - Book 1 (Gabe and Sinc's story)

A Healing Heart - Book 2 (Ethan and Hana's story)

Book 3 releasing in 2019

Winter Solstice Wishes A Short Story in the Rogues Inc. World. (Also Book 7.5 in the Rogues Shifter Series)

Triad Series: Breaking Out, Falling Out, & Spinning Out

Rogues Shifter on Audiobook: Performed by Reba Buhr

Rebirth – Click here for samples of all my audiobooks

Stalked

Twisted

Blown Away

Caught Between

Torn Apart

Cut Off -December, 2018

BOOKS BY MARIE BOOTH:

GAYLE ALSO WRITES SPICY ROMANCE BOOKS UNDER THIS PEN NAME.

Contemporary Romance:

The Gate Series: A sexy contemporary series surrounding members of an exclusive club for men.

Stroke: Book 1

Simmer: Book 2

Split: Book 3 releases spring, 2019

Snap: Book 4 releases fall, 2019

Paranormal Romance/Urban Fantasy

The Steamy Bites Series:

Dying for a Bite – a funny contemporary vampire ménage. Think Buffy meets "Say Yes to the Dress" with some Sookie sprinkles on top.

Worst Holiday Ever Anthology:

My story - Ringing in the Reefer- Set in the Steamy Bites world

The Theta Series: A post apocalyptic series set in NYC

Playing with Passion

Yielding to Pleasure

Forgotten Shifter Series

Banished - Coming in 2019 A spicy hot Gay shifter novella

Connect to Marie

To subscribe to Marie's newsletter or find out more about her books, you can go here:

Website: http://www.mariebooth.com

Facebook: http://facebook.com/marieboothbooks

Twitter: http://twitter.com/marieboothbooks

ACKNOWLEDGMENTS

I'd like to thank my daughters and my brother for their continued love and support. A huge shout out also goes to the wonderful members of the Silicon Valley chapter of RWA. I'd never have been able to write my stories without the inspiration I get at every meeting. Supreme gratitude to Debbie Williams and Emily Schiller for their editing skills. And a ton of very special love and thanks goes out to the Le Bou Crew for their patience and encouragement.

Winter Solstice Wishes Cover Design: Tatiana Villa http://www.viladesign.net/

And to my readers: You help my world and my characters come to life. I appreciate you so very much. Thank you from my heart.

Connect to Gayle (She loves to hear from readers)
Website: http://www.gayleparness.com
Facebook: http://facebook.com/gayleparnessauthor
Twitter: http://twitter.com/gayleparness
Instagram:

Goodreads: https://www.goodreads.com/author/show/5165431.Gayle_Parness?from_search=true

Bookbub: https://www.bookbub.com/authors/gayle-parness

Subscribe to Gayle's newsletter for the latest news about her books and fun contests: https://www.gayleparness.com